David McKee

Red Fox

It was a very, very windy day. Elmer, the patchwork elephant, was sheltering in a cave with his elephant friends, some birds and Cousin Wilbur, who was playing tricks with his voice. The elephants laughed when Wilbur made his voice come from a hole at the back of the cave.

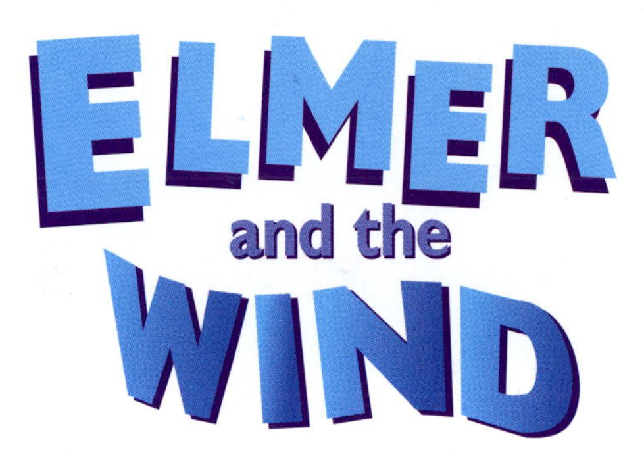
ELMER
and the
WIND

In memory of Barbara -
with love and thanks for Chantel, Chuck and Brett

A RED FOX BOOK : 0 09 940263 7

First published in Great Britain by Andersen Press Ltd 1997

Red Fox edition published 1999

9 10 8

Red Fox Books are published by Random House Children's Books,
61-63 Uxbridge Road, London W5 5SA,
a division of The Random House Group Ltd,
in Australia by Random House Australia (Pty) Ltd,
20 Alfred Street, Milsons Point, Sydney, NSW 2061, Australia
in New Zealand by Random House New Zealand Ltd,
18 Poland Road, Glenfield, Auckland 10, New Zealand
and in South Africa by Random House (Pty) Ltd,
Endulini, 5A Jubilee Road, Parktown 2193, South Africa

THE RANDOM HOUSE GROUP Limited Reg No. 954009
www.**kidsatrandomhouse**.co.uk/elmer

A CIP catalogue record for this book is available from the British Library.

Printed in Hong Kong

“It’s not a good day for flying,” said a bird.

“It’s a good day to be a heavy elephant,” chuckled Elmer. “An elephant can’t be blown away.”

“I bet even you are afraid to go out in this wind, Elmer,” said the bird.

“Afraid?” said Elmer. “Watch this then. Come on, Wilbur.”

“Come back, don’t be silly,” called the elephants.

But Elmer and Wilbur had already gone out into the wind.

Once they were behind some trees and out of sight of the others, Elmer led the way into another cave.

"You're up to something, Elmer," said Wilbur.

"Yes," laughed Elmer. "Make your voice come from

out there as if we were still walking away. Sound like me sometimes."

"I get it," said Wilbur. His voice came from the distance, sounding like Elmer, "It's hard to move in this wind." Then like himself, "Careful, Elmer, hold on."

The elephants heard the voices and started to worry.
Wilbur called, "Hold on to something, Elmer. Look out!"

"HELP!" came Elmer's voice. "HELP! I'm flying."
Wilbur called, "ELMER! COME BACK! ELMER!
OH, HELP! HELP!"

"Elmer's being blown away, we must help," said an elephant.

"If you go out you'll be blown away too," said a bird.

"Form a chain, trunks holding tails," said another elephant.

They crept out of the cave, each elephant holding the tail of the elephant in front.

"Look at them," said Elmer. "They do look funny."

"Come back, you'll be blown away," called Wilbur.

The elephants all started to speak at once, but because they were holding on with their trunks, their voices sounded very strange:

"We've been fooled!"

"The rotters . . ."

"It's an Elmer and Wilbur trick."

Then they backed back into the cave and looked funnier than ever.

When they were safely back in the cave, Elmer and Wilbur returned as well. The elephants enjoyed the joke but a bird said, "That was very silly, Elmer."

"But really, Bird," said Elmer, "an elephant can't be blown away. I'll walk to those trees and back to prove it."

"Another trick," said an elephant, as Elmer walked away.

They watched as Elmer disappeared behind some trees.

Then they heard Elmer's voice calling, "Help! I can't keep on the ground."

The elephants laughed, "Very funny, Wilbur."

The voice came again, "HELP! I'M FLYING!"

The elephants laughed louder than ever.

"It's not me this time," said Wilbur.

“Look!” said a bird. “It isn’t Wilbur.”
The elephants stared: there was Elmer above the trees.
“What’s he doing up there?” gasped an elephant.
“It’s called flying,” said a bird.
“Poor Elmer,” said an elephant.

"It's my ears," thought Elmer. "They're acting as wings."
Wilbur and the others seemed very small as he flew away.

“This is really quite fun,” thought Elmer after a while. He could see the other animals sheltering from the wind. They stared to see an elephant fly by.

“It’s Elmer,” said a lion. “I expect he’s up to another of his tricks.”

At last the wind dropped and Elmer landed.
"Oh dear," he thought. "It's going to be a long walk home. It serves me right for being so silly."

When the wind stopped, the birds flew off to find Elmer and help guide him home. When at last the elephants saw the birds flying above the trees, they knew that Elmer was near. They rushed to meet him to hear about his adventure.

“You were wrong, Elmer,” said the bird. “An elephant can be blown away.”

“You were wrong, too, Bird,” laughed Elmer. “It was a lovely day for flying!”

Some
besteslling Red Fox
picture books

THE BIG ALFIE AND ANNIE ROSE STORYBOOK
by Shirley Hughes

OLD BEAR
by Jane Hissey

OI! GET OFF OUR TRAIN
by John Burningham

GORGEOUS!
by Caroline Castle and Sam Childs

NOT NOW, BERNARD
by David McKee

ALL JOIN IN
by Quentin Blake

JESUS' CHRISTMAS PARTY
by Nicholas Allan

WHERE THE WILD THINGS ARE
by Maurice Sendak

EAT YOUR PEAS
by Kes Gray and Nick Sharratt

THE RUNAWAY TRAIN
By Benedict Blathwayt

Spectacular new prints take inspiration from Turkish tiles and Persian carpets

Discover the decade that gave fashion the mini skirt, Op Art prints, and the discotheque dress in this super-cool coloring book created by fashion aficionado, Iain R. Webb.

$12.99 US | $14.99 CAN

ISBN 978-1-84091-744-4

9 781840 917444

WWW.OCTOPUSBOOKSUSA.COM

Picture credits:

All drawings, by Iain R. Webb, are based on images by the following photographers © The Condé Nast Publications Ltd.

Clive Arrowsmith 50, 73
Cecil Beaton 11, 57, 58, 85
John Chan 18
Henry Clarke 7, 14, 17, 19, 21, 36, 45, 47, 49, 52, 55, 56, 59, 63, 65, 68, 71, 72, 74, 84, 86, 90, 91, 92, 93
John Cowan 38
Jerry Czember 69
Arnaud de Rosnay 32
Justin de Villeneuve 79
Brian Duffy 10, 20, 24, 26, 40, 41, 48, 51, 60, 80, 94
Norman Eales 43, 62, 66
Frank Horvat 35
Patrick Hunt 23
Just Jaeckin front cover, 15, 16
Peter Knapp 77
Barry Lategan 37, 70, 88, 95
Jeanloup Sieff 28, 46
Sandra Lousada 34
David Montgomery 2, 4, 13, 25, 29, 64, 76, 78, 81, 87, back cover
Harri Peccinotti 61
Peter Rand 9, 12, 33, 82
Franco Rubartelli 8
Donald Silverstein 89
David Stanford 75
Ronald Traeger 1, 6, 22, 30, 31, 44, 83
Eugene Vernier 27, 39, 42, 53, 54

Front Cover:
April 15 1967
YOUNG IDEA SAYS IT'S A GREAT YEAR FOR DADDY-LONG-LEGS

Back Cover:
May 1966
THE TWO FACES OF BEAUTY: SAVAGE AND ROMANTIC

An Hachette UK Company
www.hachette.co.uk

First published in Great Britain in 2016 by Conran Octopus Ltd, a division of Octopus Publishing Group Ltd, Carmelite House
50 Victoria Embankment
London EC4Y 0DZ
www.octopusbooksusa.com

Distributed in the US by Hachette Book Group
1290 Avenue of the Americas
4th and 5th Floors
New York, NY 10020

Distributed in Canada by
Canadian Manda Group
664 Annette St.
Toronto, Ontario, Canada M6S 2C8

ISBN 978 1 84091 744 4

Printed and bound in China
10 9 8 7 6 5 4 3 2 1

Publisher: Alison Starling
Creative Director: Jonathan Christie
Assistant Editor: Ella Parsons
Proofreader: Jane Ellis
Senior Production Manager: Katherine Hockley

Author's Acknowledgements:
I would very much like to thank the team at Conran Octopus, including Ella Parsons, Jane Ellis, and Katherine Hockley, for making this book possible, particularly Alison Starling for her continued enthusiasm and dedication to the project. I have enjoyed working with Jonathan Christie whose sophisticated art direction has made my original idea into such a glamtastic book. I look forward to working with Ellen Bashford and Frances Teehan, always a pleasure. I would also like to thank the team at Condé Nast Publications Ltd, including Alexandra Shulman, Brett Croft, and Nicky Eaton. I am indebted to Roseanne Lau for her tireless and exacting organization of the project and Harriet Wilson, who has become a fierce conspirator and fine friend. Thanks also to Julian Alexander. As ever, I would like to thank Rosemary Harden at the Fashion Museum, Bath, for her continued support and expert eye, along with access to their wonderful collection; also Central St Martin's and London College of Fashion for use of their libraries. Once again, I could not have made this book without Gregory Davis, who shares my love of fabulous frocks, and Mark Clarke, who helped with the hairstyles. I would especially like to thank all the wonderful *Vogue Coloring Book* fans around the world who have shared their amazing interpretations of my illustrations on Instagram. I am thrilled that they are coloring with such panache.

I dedicate this book to my sister Mary.
I miss her.

ENJOY COLORING YOUR OWN *VOGUE* COVER

#VOGUEGOESPOP

VOGUE